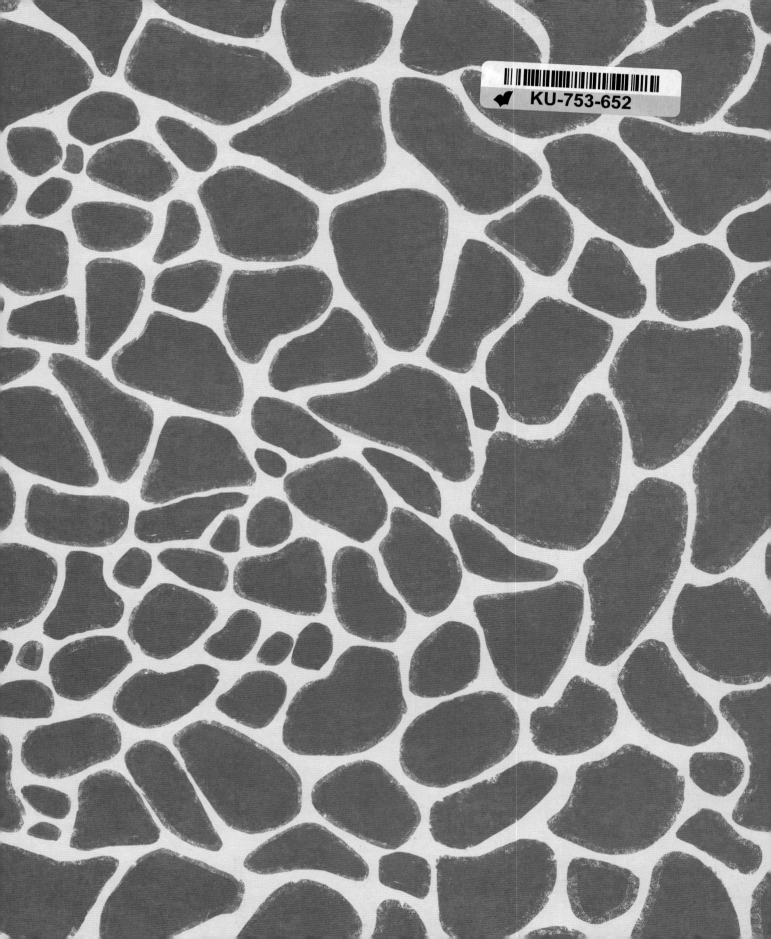

To Erin Ruth… because friendships come
in all shapes and sizes   S.J.D.

To my friends – my "lovable girls". Without you
and your diversity my life would be trivial!   G.C.

Text copyright © 2017 Sarah J. Dodd
Illustrations copyright © 2017 Giusi Capizzi
This edition copyright © 2019 Lion Hudson IP Limited

The right of Sarah J. Dodd to be identified as the author and of Giusi Capizzi to be identified as the illustrator
of this work has been asserted by them in accordance with the Copyright, Designs and Patents Act 1988.

Published by
Lion Hudson Limited
Wilkinson House, Jordan Hill Business Park,
Banbury Road, Oxford OX2 8DR, England
www.lionhudson.com

Paperback ISBN 978 0 7459 7713 3

First edition 2019

A catalogue record for this book is available from the British Library

Printed and bound in Malaysia, February 2019, LH18

Just Like You

Miki the meerkat makes a friend

Sarah J. Dodd

Illustrated by Giusi Capizzi

LION
CHILDREN'S

Miki and Mama peeped over the fence.

"What's going on?" said Miki.

"A new family is moving in next door," said the keeper.

"Will there be anyone for me to play with?" asked Miki.

"Yes," said the keeper. "A new friend called Raffa. She's just like you."

Miki was so excited that he couldn't stay still.

"A new friend!" he chattered. "And she's just like me! I can't wait to play with her."

The next morning, Miki couldn't wait to get outside.

He looked all around, but the new friend was nowhere to be seen.

Instead, there were four grey hooves, four enormous legs, and something was blocking out the sun.

Miki looked up… and up… and up…

"Hello," said a tall voice from somewhere in the sky. "I'm Raffa."
"No, no," said Miki. "There must be some mistake. You can't be my friend."
"Why not?" said Raffa.

"I sleep in a burrow, curled in a ball," said Miki. "You sleep in a shed, standing up. You're nothing like me."

"Well," said Raffa, "*You* eat food off the floor.

I eat fresh green leaves from the treetops. You're nothing like *me*."

"I'm very small," said Miki.
"You're ever so, *ever so* tall.
You're nothing like me."

"I talk to birds soaring in the sky," said Raffa.

"You talk to bugs crawling on the ground.
You're nothing like *me*."

"You can't be my friend," said Miki.
He turned his back.
  "And you can't be *my* friend," said Raffa.
She turned her back, too.

"I mean it," said Miki, sticking his nose in the air. "And I mean it, too," said Raffa, sticking *her* nose in the air.

Night fell, and Mama called Miki back into the burrow.

"It's time for bed," she said.

"Not yet," said Miki. "I'm not sleepy, not at all. I want to go and watch the wide, white moon."

He waited until Mama was snoozing, then crept outside.

But somebody else was already there…

"What are you doing here?" asked Miki.

"I can't sleep," said Raffa, shaking her heavy head.

"Just like me," said Miki. "I want to watch the wide, white moon."

"Just like me!" said Raffa. "I want to watch the wide, white moon, too!"

"But that's not fair," said Miki. "Watching the moon was my idea."

"No it wasn't," said Raffa. "Watching the moon was *my* idea."

They looked up at the blue-black sky.
 "Where *is* the moon?" they said together.
But there was no moon.
Instead, there was…

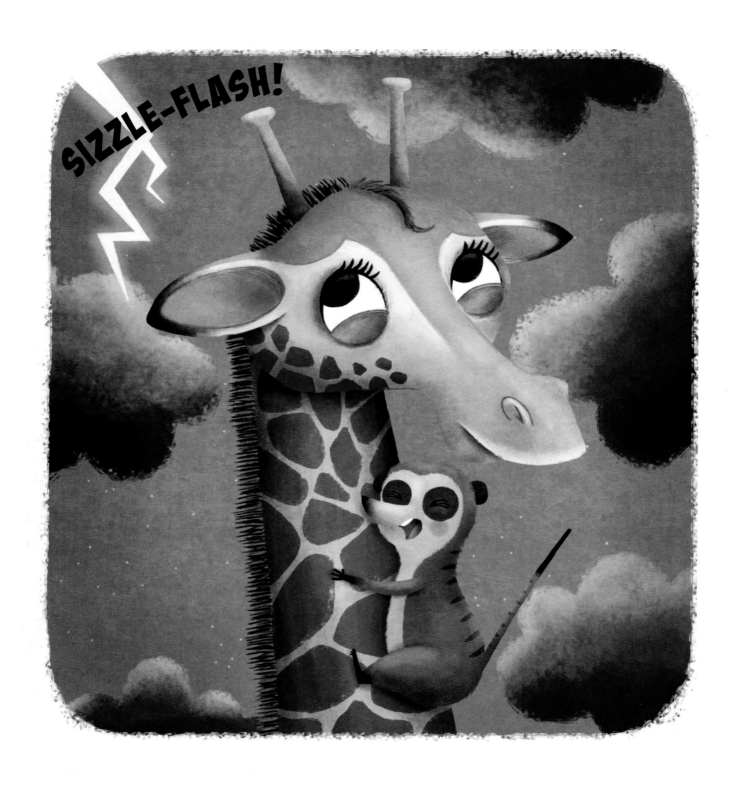

"I'm scared of lightning!" cried Miki.
"Just like me," whimpered Raffa.

"I'm scared of thunder!" cried Raffa.

"Just like me," whimpered Miki.

They shivered and shook, and clung together until the storm had passed.

"I've never seen the world from up here," said Miki.
"It's so beautiful!"

"And I've never seen the world from down here," said
Raffa. "It's so interesting!"

Miki and Raffa played together all night long.

Miki showed Raffa how to catch bugs on her tongue.

Raffa showed Miki how to choose the sweetest, juiciest leaves.

They giggled and jiggled until the wide, white moon faded into morning.

At last, Mama came out.

"*Now* it's time for bed," she said.

"But I want to play with my new friend," said Miki, with a yawn.

"Raffa needs her sleep," said Mama with a smile…

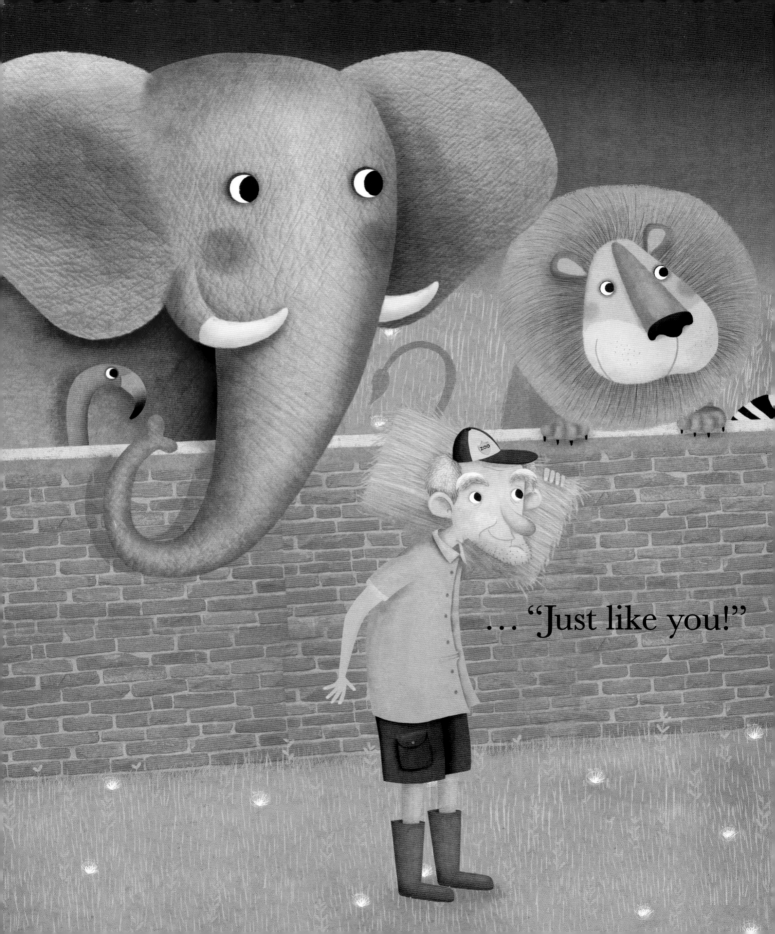

… "Just like you!"

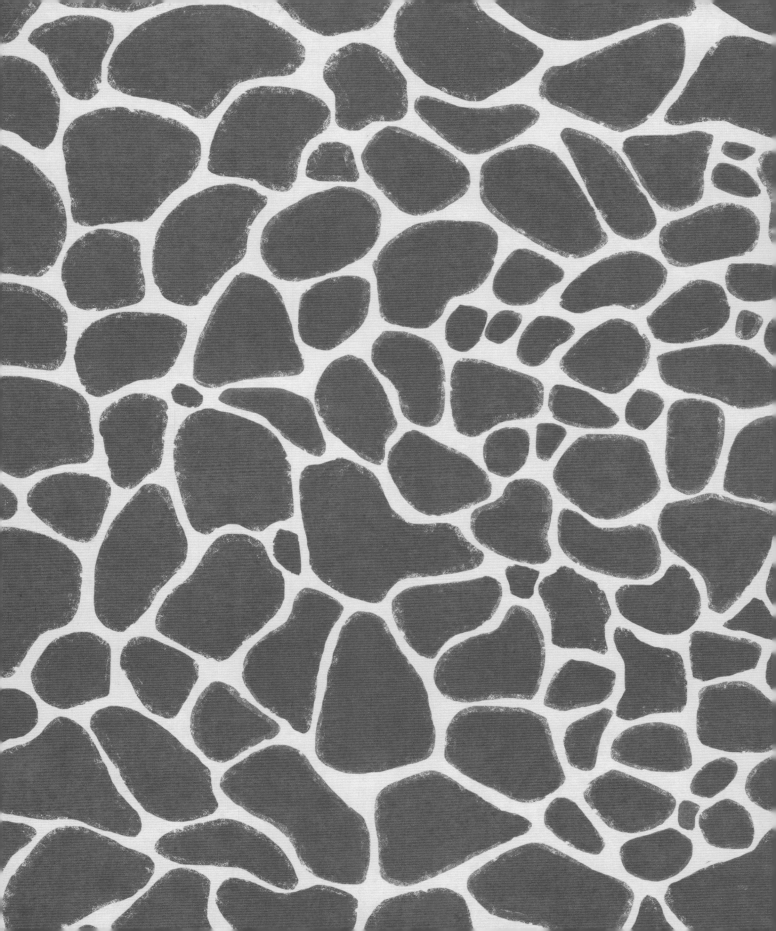

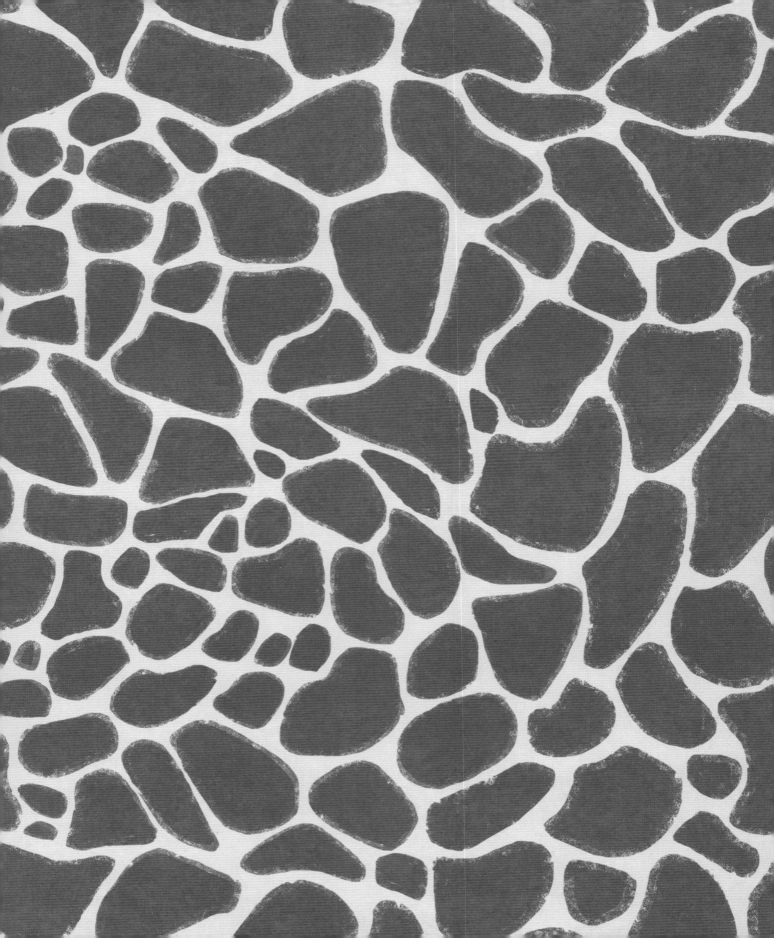

Other titles from Lion Children's Books

Legs *Sarah J. Dodd*

I Want a Friend *Anne Booth*

My Stinky New School *Rebecca Elliott*

Hogs Hate Hugs *Tiziana Bendall-Brunello & John Bendall-Brunello*

Missing Jack *Rebecca Elliott*

Magnus *Claire Shorrock*